Quirky the Porcupine

By Maureen Friedman illustrated by Dani Williams

For my daughter, who has
all my love.

Quirky the porcupine loved to wake to the sunbeams as they crept into his room. He enjoyed walking through a daisy field on a quiet afternoon.

In the evening, after supper, he would read about distant islands. He wouldn't say goodnight, because he was a porcupine no one befriends.

Porcupines, you see, are usually nocturnal, so they sleep in the daytime. But Quirky was different, his prickles got cold, so he liked the sunshine.

So while all the other porcupines laid their heads down
to sleep, Quirky was just getting up on his feet.

He often felt lonely; he often felt sad. Why did everyone
think that the sunshine was bad?

All Quirky wanted was a friend he could hug who could
keep him warm and make him feel safe and snug.

Therefore he went on a mission, to find a new friend…
even if it took him to earth's very end.

But it was tough finding a good friend, you see, because
Quirky was covered in quills that were rather prickly.

Quirky nearly gave up; his eyes filled with blue tears.
Would he be alone for the rest of his years?

Sadly he rested; his search had left him plum-tuckered.
When suddenly, to his surprise, he spotted a butterfly
whose mouth was quite puckered.

She fluttered about, with many to's and fro's, finally
landing on Quirky's button-y nose.

"Hello," she said, "My name is Posy." And she gave
him a kiss that turned his cheeks very rosy.

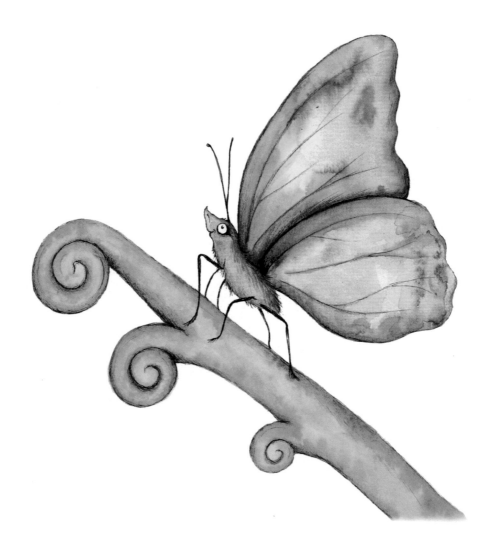

Quirky had been searching so long for a hug; he hadn't
considered this little flying bug.

With a hug quite impossible, Posy had given Quirky a tiny little kiss. He had not realized what before he had missed!

It just goes to show you that every pot has its lid. For butterflies & porcupines, kisses were better, so that's just what they did.

Maureen is a child at heart and the author of Quirky
The Porcupine and several other forthcoming tales for
children. She lives in Frederick, MD with her husband
and daughter. She enjoys travel and watching the sun
set over the mountains from her front porch.

Made in the USA
Middletown, DE
01 May 2018